Sco scha

nüglia nu

fuss

Translated from Romansh

As If Nothing Were
Rut Plouda

Translated from Romansh by
Hannah Felce

First published in English by Strangers Press, Norwich, 2022
part of UEA Publishing Project

First published in original language by Octopus, 2000
Published by Chasa Editura Rumantscha, 2014

All rights reserved
Author © Rut Plouda, 2000
Translator © Hannah Felce, 2022

Printed by
Swallowtail, Norwich

Series editors
Nathan Hamilton & Lucy Rand

Editorial assistance
Lily Alden, Erin Maniatopoulou and Emma Seager

Proofread by
Senica Maltese

Cover design and typesetting
Glen Robinson (aka GRRR.UK)

Design Copyright © Glen Robinson, 2022

The rights of Rut Plouda to be identified as the author and
Hannah Felce to be identified as the translator of this work
have been asserted in accordance with the Copyright, Designs
and Patents Act, 1988. This booklet is sold subject to the
condition that it shall not, by way of trade or otherwise, be lent,
resold, hired out, stored in a retrieval system, or otherwise
circulated without the publisher's prior consent in any form
of binding or cover other than that in which it is published
and without a similar condition including this condition being
imposed on the subsequent purchaser.

ISBN: 978-1-913861-48-3

Rut Plouda

As
If
Nothing
Were

UEA
PUBLISHING
PROJECT

strangers press

TRANSLATED by HANNAH FELCE

THE TRAIN PASSES, TWISTING AND TURNING UP the valley. Joannes had taken his bag and gone. It was dark by the time he left the village.

The trains come and go.

The train approaches, twisting and turning down the valley. Joannes arrives. He places his bag on the floor and cries out with joy.
  The train is red.

The train is waiting. People at the station walk back and forth. Joannes drops into his mother's arms.
    The trains come and go.

✹

The Alpine choughs have arrived over the rooftops, a black swarm, and have scattered across the gutter, across the summerhouse, across the acer tree. I've placed a bowl of leftovers on the staircase banister outside. They are there, waiting. It continues to snow. The cars pass noiselessly. They drive between the white edges of the road, as if doing something forbidden. As soon as I go into the house, the choughs fly onto the banister. I hear the dark, heavy strokes of their wings. They fight, push each other away, quickly fill their beaks and dart off. More arrive and push their way forward with shrill calls. A short while later, the bottom of the bowl is covered in fresh snow, as are the crumbs that have fallen to the ground. The choughs have vanished.

    The cacti on the kitchen windowsill hardly reach the frame. I give them a little water and think of the desert. I think of the colour of the sand, the rocks, the smell of the caravans. I like the desert, yet do not know it. I water my cacti every so often, mop up what I have spilt, and notice that outside it is winter.

✹

It is warm in the stables. I pick up the rake, clean the cows' stall, and then the one for the youngstock. I see you picking up the pitchfork to scatter hay. It is hard work, but you do not pause. You are your father, driving the fork into the pile of hay and drawing it back before the mangers. You are your father, climbing the barn ladder, picking up the cold hay knife and pushing it into the haystack with your foot until the slices drop to the ground and break up. You are your father, wearing overalls, leading the sheep from the stables to the fountain, and leaning on your stick while you wait. It is the depths of winter, it gets dark early, and the stars are already out. I watch the lambs leaping in the snow while the ewes drink greedily. Then the herd trots back up into the stables. A familiar pattern is left in the snow around the fountain and up the street. The light is still on in the henhouse. The hens are all sitting on the perch. One tilts her head to the side and makes a strange sound.

✺

There are words that remain or become unfamiliar. That cannot pass through the door. That are left behind somewhere in the hospital hallway. PERSONALBELONGINGS, for example:

- ✺ a winter jacket
- ✺ a jumper with a cut down its front
- ✺ a pair of grey trousers
- ✺ a pair of dark blue boxer shorts
- ✺ a vest with a cut down its front
- ✺ a pair of grey socks
- ✺ a pair of boots lined with sheepskin
- ✺ a grey woollen scarf
- ✺ a bag containing a gold necklace, earrings, a wristwatch
- ✺ a bum bag containing a wallet, an identity card, a multi-trip train ticket with five dates, times and places stamped on it.

PERSONALBELONGINGS. In a paper bag that I am suddenly holding in my hands. That I am placing in the car. That I am carrying into the house.

✺

It is windy and stormy. There is something fresh and unsettled moving through the village today. There is tension in everything, a sense of alertness. The chimes of the church bell fall bare into the flurry of snow. I close the window and warm my hands by the stove. In the living room, it smells of mandarins and chocolate, and a little of the washing I hung up to dry. All that is missing now is the tapping of the shutter. Everything seems new to me. Just like when I moved here. Everything was different. Even winter. Even the songs. And then there were those starry nights with the calm, clear mountains. Nights that numbed your face. Your father and I were a prince and princess, the snow crunching underfoot.

L'amour, ça fait pleurer, that is how the song went, but love made us laugh, allowed us to fly through days and nights.

L'amour, ça fait pleurer.

※

The train window is covered in clusters of snow. Sometimes a drop of water slides in between them, downwards at first, then unexpectedly changes course, back or forth, and comes to a halt. It is dark outside and still snowing. The train stops at every station. I do not see all these changes on the window, nor do I hear the train's dull strokes every time it starts moving again. My gaze is directed at the window when, all of a sudden, I'm in our living room, with the candle lit on the sill, the cat stretched out on the stove, books and newspapers on the floor. The telephone rings, here I am, you say, and I try to remember your voice. The window is back. Something has changed, but what, I do not know. You like watching the tunnels approaching. You are sitting on the seat cross-legged, and while dark walls thunder past outside, you feel courageous and strong and there is a sparkle in your eye.

The train jolts forward and my plastic bag falls to the ground. The man's voice coming from the loudspeaker states the name of the next station. It sounds like an accusation.

THE SHEPHERD

The moment the shepherd picks up a stick, he is walking through the village streets behind a flock of sheep, which is visibly growing. He hears the bleating of the ewes that have lost their little ones, and the bleating of the lambs looking for their mothers. Children, men and women are standing in front of the houses and stables. They call out. They shout. They laugh. The flock leaves the village. All is left behind: faces, hands, voices. The shepherd sees only his flock, how it is growing, softening. He follows it, he leads it. His day is filled with sunshine, bells and the bleating of the sheep. The shepherd is not afraid of the dark. He has his dog, his fire and his pocketknife. The herd is resting and ruminating. He cuts slices of bread and cheese and shares them with his dog. The fire is big. A cold wind is blowing up from the valley. The shepherd slides closer to the fire and lifts his coat collar. Below, there is the sound of rushing water. Above, there are stars and stars.

※

What distinguishes Sunday from the other days of the week? I wake up, I think Sunday, today is Sunday, and the sun outside is different as the church bell chimes seven o'clock. Snippets of dreams float through my mind, appointments for this upcoming Monday or last Friday, the feeling of being indebted to someone creeps up for a moment. Later I hear music coming from your room: Eine Herde weisser Schafe ist mein Königreich, a herd of white sheep is my kingdom... CDs and cassette tapes are scattered on the floor. The drawer of your bedside table is half open. You have taken out postcards containing holiday messages: Greece, Rimini, Paris. You look at them, the postcards, and say nothing. Then you put them away and start getting dressed... und die kleine Hütte mein Palast, and the little hut is my palace. Every time the song ends, you press the button and it starts over again. I look at the posters that you have hung up on your wall, the faces, the bodies. You sit on the edge of your bed and put on your socks. One day, you say, I'm going away. I'm going to sail away on a boat on the sea and never return.

☀

Snow is melting everywhere. Your father is collecting hazel catkins. They look good next to the wooden sign with your name on it. On the other side of the wall, it still smells of goats. The path up the slope is clear of snow now and covered in snail shells. Sometimes I sit on the bench, but not for long. The wind is still rather cold. Snow or frost returns to the village every night.

Not long ago, I saw you on your bedroom windowsill, you were gazing out through the closed window. You stared for a long while up at the grey sky. Spring was nowhere to be seen, not on the mountains, not in the woods, not even down in the yard. Your father had let the sheep out in the yard. There was still ice in the wooden fountain. The lambs were jumping around, and the ewes were ramming each other or letting their lambs suckle. They then started bleating to be let back into the barn and continue feeding.

The acer is bare. Only dried leaves and fruit from last year still hang on its branches. When the acer is restless, some of its little propellors become detached and fall in circular motions to the ground. Tomorrow or the day after, the lilac shrub will be covered in light-green buds. For now, it stands there, leaning against the garden fence, as if nothing were changing.

☀

It is sunny outside. I have closed the yellow curtain over the balcony door. The edge of its fabric casts wave-like shadows across the bottom of the window pane. The snow is melting on the roof and its droplets fall from the gutter onto the balcony floor. I cannot see the wet concrete outside, but when the droplets splash to the ground, it seems as if something is resisting them, as if they are being pushed back a little, and I am reminded of how hens move when they are pecking at grains strewn on the ground, a litany of peckpeckpeck.

The sun moves behind the wood; the droplets fall less frequently. I like the yellow of the curtain, and the yellow of the chrysanthemums on your grave, and the yellow of the postman's van, which stops in front of me. You are walking towards me, someone calls out, and approaching the house, you ask what's for dinner.

※

A whiff of hot oil, the smell of pommes frites, is enough to remind me of the round table, with the village youth, the smoke, the beer glasses with foam around the edges. The tables are well-occupied, it is a Friday or Saturday night. The sounds of everyone talking and laughing, eating and drinking, mingle with the hiss of the coffee machine and the occasional interjection of the till. It is hot, but you still have your leather jacket on. Every so often, you all stand up to say 'cheers,' and it gets louder. You belong here. And when you pay, you put the banknote on the table with a thud.

During the night, I hear you get out of a car, open the front door, and climb the stairs. A slither of light from the attic shines through the gap at the bottom of our door. Outside our window is the acer. I cannot see it, but I know it is there, motionless.

THE SAILOR

The sailor leaves the house without saying a word.
    He has left behind his dog, his box of cassettes and the palm tree in front of his bedroom window. Once he is on the boat, the men lift the anchor and the boat leaves the port with a long, monotonal sound. How vast the ocean. The boat sails on and on. The sailor stands legs astride at the bridge. He laughs and curses with his companions and spits on the floor. Sometimes, when the ocean is particularly calm, one of his dreams fumbles through the depths of the water and surfaces with a conch. It shines in the sunlight. Can you hear them sing, the sailors? They smell of tar, fish and salt. The boat keeps sailing further and further away, until all that remains is the ocean.

You know everything here: the path that sometimes loses itself among the pastures, the sticks and dry branches scattered around, the little hills and trenches, the stones, and the pond, small and partly overgrown, enclosed by a wooden fence. From a distance, I can already hear the males' calls. Once I arrive at the fence and lean on one of the planks, it becomes quiet. I stand still and wait. There are toads and frogs everywhere, one on top of the other, but motionless. For a moment, the pond seems enchanted. But then there is movement, a coming, a going, a vanishing. A couple of females are swimming with males on their backs. There are brown leaves in the pond, on its bank a dead toad lying on its back. A little further away, a frog jumps into the water and the dead toad moves. From between the reeds, the monotone cries resume, rising, subsiding, rising again. This time last year the pond was still frozen. Yet the toads and frogs had broken through the ice. They were scattered in the snow; little, dark, motionless piles.
    When I walk over to the River En, you are already there. It is summer and midday, and a rubber dinghy sails by with singing men

on board. You stand there, watching. Then, one of the men throws a red ball in our direction. We try to catch it, but it slips through our fingers and into the water, floating away along the riverbank.

※

In the train, there is a smell of unease. It is wafting in through the window. The carriage is nearly empty. At the back, someone is rustling around in a paper bag. A girl is listening to music on a Walkman. I can only hear the monotone boom, boom, boom. I close my eyes and lean my head on the headrest. Boom, boom, boom. Even the music smells. Everything has its own smell: days, sounds, moments. The two hours between five and seven o'clock when the Croatian lady cooks her cabbage dish, for example. The smell fills the apartment, creeps up the walls, comes up through the floor, and even spreads into the apartment above, folds itself around the stuffed elephant hung on the ceiling, around the fruit bowl on the table, around the faces on the photographs, and seeps into the blue bedroom curtains. And the hours spent up in front of the open chest in the attic that smell old. It is a smell that pierces the eyes and hands, which instantly makes you feel almost drunk on so much that has passed, on so much unknown and yet familiar.

And from afar, the smell of Sundays: woollen socks hanging on the back of the stove, the male choir's Credo and Sanctus, roast and mashed potatoes, and evenings asking questions that have something to do with, even though we do not know exactly what, the water down in the valley and the stars high above the church.

※

The living room window is open. Someone is splitting wood outside. A rooster's crowing can be heard through the trickling of the gutter. The sparrows are squabbling in the acer. A tractor approaches. Two tractors. They pass by and the other sounds return. Cowbells sound from the stables, then a woman calls out to a child who responds.

A car comes and goes. Another tractor. The wind blows the

smell of manure through the window. A minute of a day in April.

It is dark and cold in the hallway. I go to the front door. The cat is stretched out on the slabs in front of the house. His fur glistens. The sun warms my face, my hands, my belly. I close my eyes and the sun is a word. I see it, I say it. It becomes more and more foreign. Its sound, its shape, it all seems new; a word I have only just discovered. SUN. And it is already down by the River En, warming the sand, so much so that after a while we need to retreat to the shade. Here are trees and rocks, rubber dinghies with men and women aboard, waving and shouting and laughing and sailing past each other. And you are laughing, searching for your camera.

In winter, when the En silently flows between its banks, we will see these men and women in their bright outfits on the screen on our living room wall.

✺

I think 'sea' and you are on your knees, collecting sand and building towers and caves with your friends. Behind you, the waves slide away from the shore and take back the seashells that you placed there — and give, and take, and give, and take.

I think 'surface of the sea' and we are on the balcony, looking out at the water, and for a moment, we know that the seagull's cry changes the sea.

I think 'surface' and I think mirror and you are looking at your reflection and you say 'damned mongoloid'.

✺

While eating dinner, the wind wrenches at the birch tree, batters raindrops onto the window and entwines in a strange dance with the blossoming lilac bush. The clock tower chimes half past the hour. Now you are walking down the lane and opening the front door. I hear your footsteps in the hallway. You are mumbling to yourself. Outside on the balcony, the clothes horse with the washing on it has fallen over. A little while later, the wind settles and the sun appears.

The raindrops glitter on the birch tree's leaves, and the redstart flies onto a branch. Even the swallows start flying around again. They built their nest above your bedroom window once, and in autumn they flew away without us noticing. When I sit on the little cemetery wall, I have a good view of them flying up and down. They dart right past my head and fly away just above the graves.

    I stay until I hear the chiming of the evening bells. The children's voices disappear. The wind is among the firs when I leave down the path.

THE SOLDIER

I d'eiran trais sudats chi gnivan da la guerra, rum e rum e pitipum, chi gnivan da la guerra. There were once three soldiers who returned from war, *rum e rum e pitipum*, who returned from war.

※

He stomps up and down the hallway. Up and down. *Rum e rum e pitipum*. With his knapsack on his back and rifle hung over his shoulder. Soldiers rarely laugh. But they are laughing on the train. And in the pub, with a bottle of beer in hand. They hold it and make noise, tell jokes and burp. They also laugh when they are lying in the sun on their backs in the field, their hands folded under their heads. They mess around, close their eyes and open them a little when a shadow passes over. Soldiers on television do not mess around. They lie on their fronts and aim. They run and die. Up with their rifle, down with their rifle, up and down the hallway. The soldier. The soldiers. All the soldiers.

※

Ed ün da quels trais portaiva üna rösa. And one of the three wore a rose.

※

The soldier goes out of the front door and watches the men unload bales of straw. The cloud of dust makes them cough a little. The men are working fast. They squeeze their fingers underneath the string, lift the bales with a jolt, turn and throw them off the wagon. One takes out a tissue, cleans his nose, wipes away the sweat from his face and neck, and grabs another bale. His arms are strong. Little pieces of straw stick to his hair.

The rose is still closed, its petals closely nestled next to one another, soft and red.

The dog is calm while the soldier moves his hand through his fur. Back and forth, the hand moves, up and down. The dog is warm and soft.

The soldier is sitting on the bottom step of the attic stairs. He looks down at his feet. When soldiers are tired, they lie down wherever and sleep. They snore and dream. Rows and rows of soldiers. *Rum e rum e pitipum*... rows and rows and rows.

※

The day cautiously approaches the shore from a distance and a moment later, the lake slides under a silver cape. I stand in front of the open window and breathe in the damp air deeply. My dreams sometimes stay and unfurl repeatedly before me, blending into my day.

You rarely remember your dreams. In the morning, they flee to the corner of the room together with the night and are gone in an instant. You sit yourself up in bed, yawn, and your languid body does not quite know where to start the day. You were next to me last night, soft, silent, with an absent stare. I woke up and immediately the waters of the lake that keep flowing and flowing to the shore were there. There was splashing outside and streaming water, a mixture of sounds, strange and wet.

※

An afternoon snack laid out on a chequered blanket, sun and laughter, sand all around, stones, pastures, and the River En. Later, you are sitting barefoot on a stone. You are fishing and singing 'vieni sulla barche-e-tta'. You watch the river stream towards us, and I watch how it streams past us. I keep watching until I am a child again, and the En arrives at the wooden bridge, past the Grand Hotel with the blue shutters. Gentlemen with slightly stiff legs stroll around, ladies carry sulky dogs in their arms. Inside the hotel, red carpets lead directly to paradise. Waiters and waitresses whirl around everywhere and knock on locked doors. It smells of hot chocolate and pastries.

And outside is the park with the flowers, the greenery and the sunshine rented especially for these people strolling about in their bathrobes or sitting happily at the tables. But then winter arrives. The park is frozen, the shutters are closed. Above the Grand Hotel stands the sinister forest. At the end of the park, the En streams by. It does not like it when you peer out of the peepholes in the bridge to see how it passes by and then around the corner out of sight. The En does not begin anywhere. It ends in the sea, but the sea is so far away the En will never reach it.

※

In my memories, summer only lasts a few days. They are the days that burn on the bench by the front door and on the fields while haymaking. Down in the garden, everything is still; the colours have withdrawn a little, even the reddish orange of the fire lilies that are still in bloom. Tourists are searching for restaurants, and it smells like hay and hot engines. The heat is in the overcrowded bus and between the poppies by the roadside below the village. There are also one or two days where you feel unwell, and you are lying on the bench by the stove and remind me that we wanted to sail along the En to the Danube one day. And then come the rainy days, the fog moving up from the valley floor and lingering until the goats return home bleating, shaking themselves off before going into the stables. The signs that shine through the grey say the circus is arriving soon, and you cheer every time you spot one. Then one day you are sitting among children and adults in the dim marquee, which transforms for a few hours into a magical world. You return home with light footsteps, and for a while that whole world is in your eyes. And maybe, when you well up unexpectedly, it is because of the clowns or the loneliness of the caravans that leave the towns and cities behind.

ROBINSON I

Robinson's parrot has red and blue feathers. His eyes follow his master's every movement. They are habitual and confident movements. When an abrupt, unexpected movement occurs, the parrot is unsettled for a moment. Every day, he sits on Robinson's shoulder and accompanies him while he wanders the island. When Robinson's uneasy gaze searches for the line where the sea meets the sky, the parrot comforts him with his hard beak and rough cries. He laughs, hops and larks around.

Only at night is Robinson entirely alone, and when the waves crash all the way into his dreams, he screams and sits upright in his bed. Then he can no longer sleep. He curses the solitude and the shadows on the cave walls and waits with little hope for day to break.

ROBINSON II

Robinson lives down by the River En. In the evening, he slips into his sleeping bag. Above him is the starry sky; next to him the fast-flowing river. It flows and flows, but the stars remain. Robinson knows the stars. On certain evenings, they shine only for him, they move towards him and twinkle at him. On other evenings, they do not even notice him. They shine on as if he were not there. When he wakes, the En is still flowing, the sky is now blue and as open as the day that is just beginning. Robinson gets up, builds a fire and warms his hands. Later, he wanders up and down the riverbank and fishes. The fish thrash and writhe in his hands. When it gets too hot, he lies down in the shadow of the hazel bushes. The dead fish are in his bag, wrapped in a cloth.

ROBINSON III

Robinson lives in a tent at the edge of the clearing. His horse grazes from one forest border to another, lifts his head sometimes, then continues feeding. When Robinson returns from hunting with his kill, he whistles through the trees and his horse's ears prick up. The days and nights pass, but when the moon rises clear and full above the tips of the firs and larches, the tent opens, Robinson comes out, looks around, jumps on the horse, and rides into the forest. It is hard traversing a forest full of ditches, roots and tree trunks at night. The horse is sweating. Robinson is sweating too. He is getting more and more uneasy. Finally they reach the valley, stop, and see before them the path that winds its way down. The horse is impatient and tramps the ground. Robinson holds the reins tightly and strokes his sweaty neck.

Then she appears out of the valley. On a white horse without a saddle, holding only its mane, she thunders past in a white dress, billowing hair, comes and goes without turning her head, giving him not a single glance, gallops on and disappears. The trees and stones cast dull shadows in the moonlight.

Slowly, Robinson turns his horse around and goes home.

This time I come from above, over hills, through hollows and over hills again. Then I see the cabin a little further down below, small and brown, alone on a patch of grass scattered with dwarf mountain pines. The grassy slopes and scree on the other side of the valley are already in the shade. Here the sun still warms the cabin walls, the table and bench in front of the door, and the grey stack of firewood. You are standing, a little stooped, next to the small wooden fountain and are brushing your teeth, legs apart, hair dishevelled. The wind is blowing, as it always does towards evening, and water sputters from the spout. Next to the fence are cushions of moss, fairy thimbles, and grasses. I open the door and the shutters. The mountain fills the window. Clouds are slowly drifting beyond: a shaggy cat, two faces kissing, a huge bug, embryos. I stand outside the cabin for a long time, looking into this wild, grey and lonely valley. The scree you like so much on the other side of the valley looks like a big dry tongue split several times at the tip, creeping between the mountain pines.

    You can hear the bells of cows looking for food among the gravel and stones on the valley floor. Clouds still drift behind the mountain, but faster than before. They have claws and big open mouths. The sky is in turmoil. I remove my harmonica and play a tune for you. Meanwhile, you climb the scree, approaching the cave.

※

It is windy and the waves batter the wall more vigorously than usual. I could not paint this lake. It's just like the sunset. I can only watch and wait until all of a sudden I am sitting at the parlour table amidst the clatter of cups, plates and spoons, the sound of the chairs being pulled back and forth on the wooden floor, and the gruffness of your voice. Everyone is talking at the same time. The window is open, inside it is quite dark because of the acer outside, the sun and the smell of hay are on the windowsill, the windowpane reflects a piece of the landscape. I start playing with the window, the landscape moves. I am a girl again, standing in the kitchen in front of the open window. It is summer. Reflected in the windowpane is the slope with the church and cemetery, with the crosses that stick out above the stone wall. I move the window back and forth, the church dances, the crosses move, the sun warms my hand and my striped apron. This village is just my village, new and different.

※

From the dimness of the attic, wardrobes and drawers squint back at me, boxes and dark piles of junk beside them. In the photo album there are black-and-white pictures; serious and unfamiliar faces, rarely a hint of a smile. The drawers are still tough to open. They are full to the brim: winter clothing, dolls' clothes, masks, and carnival garb. In the big wardrobe hang coats and jackets. And here are your small, dark-red sandals with the raised insole in the heel, ankle strap and metal buckle for closing, their fronts adorned with three small holes shaped like pine kernels. Light-brown soles with worn grooves. They have lost their shape a little, your shoes, especially the left one, and the red is faded. 'Petit Shoes' is written on the soles, size 18. You can hardly see the 'P' on the right shoe anymore, nor the 'S' on the left.

※

I press the button and the train door opens. The platform is bustling with people. Someone is talking through the loudspeaker. There is a breeze, but the air is pleasant. Platform three, I read, as always, and opposite is platform two. I walk along the platform; to my left is the train, to my right the empty track. Crossing the tracks is prohibited. Only in exceptional circumstances are you given the signal to cross. So you place one foot in front of the other and feel like you are going the wrong way. The trolley for luggage and postbags next to the concrete post is empty. Behind the post is the ticket validation machine. It is orange and catches your eye as soon as you walk up the stairs. The train to Chur arrives on platform two. The voice resonates from the loudspeaker again. I walk down the stairs and through the underpass. People are rushing here too, and it is windy. The heat and noise of the traffic from up the stairs is drawing closer. Cars, bicycles and two motorbikes pass on the road. And people sit in the sunshine outside the restaurant across the road.

※

There are windrows of half-wilted grass all around, a swollen petrol can and countless insects in this heat. You walk up through the field, stop by the rocks, by the steps, walk up to the cabin and sit on the bench. You stroke your dog's head and pick up the binoculars. Perhaps there are deer somewhere on the slope opposite. Ants are running back and forth at your feet. The cabin door is open. Water is on the boil inside. While I put in the spaghetti, you stand next to me at the stove and tell me something. I do not understand what you are saying. Now go and wash your hands,
I say, and put the plates on the table.
    Later, you walk along the path to the bridge. The clouds are moving fast. Tourists appear from the valley. From a distance, they look like colourful moving dots. And then they are here and walking past you. A child turns around and stares.

※

One day, the houses on the other side of the riverbank vanished. The water reached the horizon. The fishing boat stopped not far from me. The fisherman was bending over, legs wide. His boat rocked a little. After a while, he started the engine and changed location.
    I can smell it when your father has shot and gutted an animal. The congealed blood under his fingernails. The movement of his hands in its warm stomach. The pulling, cutting and tearing. The caressing.
    And you are gilling your first fish on the kitchen table and laugh out loud.

✺

It is dark in the cabin. Only your voice can be heard, singing about a sleeping village. The houses in your song have wide facades and lit windows that slowly extinguish one after the other. The water coming from the fountain is a dark splutter, and sometimes a car's headlights glide across the roofs, the facades, and the trees scattered with drowsy birds. Someone is standing at the window, looking out into the night. It is a village with gardens and courtyards, with a church and a football pitch. The people are dreaming their dreams, and here and there someone is awake, thinking.

And above everything, like sprinkles of glitter, are the stars. For the people in the village below, they awaken something like a distant memory, until one day their lives are extinguished like the lights in their windows.

That is how your song ends, your voice lost somewhere between the buildings and the gardens.

THE HUNTER

He gathers his green hat, backpack and rifle, and walks up the trail with slow and heavy footsteps, traverses the forest, stops and looks through his binoculars. The trees, the honeysuckle, the juniper, everything is alert and still. Only the birds flutter around, unable to behave themselves. When he leaves the forest, he sighs and looks over to the other side of the valley. He measures the mountain range with his hunter's gaze, sits down and has a bite to eat. Above him are the crags, grassy slopes, gullies and screes, trails that begin and end abruptly, tufts of dry grass, roots and, every now and then, a gentian flower.

Later, he returns home with a chamois draped over his shoulder, the animal's head twisted backwards. A twig hangs out of its snout. He lays his prey on the ground in the stable courtyard and glides his hand through its fur, touches its horns, lifts a leg and nods. He will later stand with his friends around the animal, which is hanging from a hook with its head down and stomach open, and they will drink the palorma. There is a dark red patch on the floor.

※

It smells like warm earth and dry potato plants on the field. I had to wear gloves to pull out this sticky and prickly weed. At the end of every furrow there is now a pile. You are sitting watching on a horse blanket at the edge of the field. I pick up the hoe and start digging, a little to the right, a little to the left, then bend over, remove the potatoes and throw them to one side. Progress is slow. The sun is getting hotter and hotter.

You come over and leisurely begin to pick up the potatoes and place them in the bowl. You recognise people in the potatoes and laugh out loud. I laugh with you and joke and dig and cry out when I cut through yet another potato. The sweat is streaming down my face, my fingernails are torn, my back hurts. Meanwhile, you have grown tired and take a break. You then spread out our afternoon snack on the blanket and wait. On the valley floor, you can see a slither of the River En. Cars drive past above us. You look over to the other side of the valley. And you say that you never want to leave. I contemplate your hands with your broad fingernails full of dirt.

※

You know how abruptly autumn can arrive, with the first snowfall that quickly comes and goes. Yet autumn remains. It edges itself into the acer tree and redcurrant bushes. Chard is strewn across the ground, the cabbage heads are hunched up, only the sunflowers are still standing upright next to the fence. The day stays grey and does not recover from the moisture. In the afternoon, the cows come home. The goats are bleating and bleating. Children and adults are running around with sticks, dogs are barking, everywhere there are voices, bleating and mooing. And then it is all over. Cowbells can be heard from the stables.

Individual droplets fall from the acer. Lights are gradually being turned on in the houses. The smoke from chimneys trails away above the rooftops and merges with the mist.

THE MUSICIAN

People are clapping and clapping. They stand up, whistle, cheer and keep on clapping. The musician on stage has his eyes closed. His body, which is slightly bent forward, moves from side to side, back and forth, and his fingers bounce lightly over the keys of the clarinet. Among the crowd is his mother who is laughing, his father and sisters are there, as are his friends, up on their feet, the butcher with his apron and big rubber boots, and she is there too, watching him. He gradually tires. The crowd, the hall and the stage disperse. He takes his clarinet, places it in its black case, and closes the lid.

※

The gravel on the mountain trail casts long shadows. These small stones, smaller than hazelnuts, almost make me laugh with their dark shadows. The larches above have turned yellow, the rose bushes extend their ripe hips, already frozen, into the cold air. Benches stand alone against the brown of the fields.

When I cross the yard, I disturb the acer leaves that cover the damp ground. My footsteps are light under these dry shells. Yet here stands the acer, still holding on to its fruit, folded between little wings, ready to fly away. Restless is the acer between the closed earth and the sky of swallows that are no longer here.

At first, the sounds of your clarinet reach only timidly down to the yard, as if from afar. Then they crescendo, becoming louder, jumping all over the place. Snowflakes whirl around. Down in the garden the sunflowers, which are leaning towards a couple of split cabbage heads, are held up with string. Beside the house, two rosebuds are still waiting for the sun. With a sudden jolt, you open the window above. Did you see that I can make it snow, did you see? And you laugh into the wind and watch how it rouses the snowflakes, making them whirl apart. Then you close the living room window and I close the garden gate, and winter arrives overnight.

✺

In the Advent scene in the window, white snowflakes hang in front of a house with brightly lit windows. In this house, you could spread a white tablecloth over the table, lay out porcelain crockery and light the candles; perhaps take down a picture that you no longer liked, or furtively look for something in the mirror. You could open the window and greet someone who was passing by. Or close the shutters and leave. You could also die in this house; leave behind the photographs on the wall, the earthenware pitcher on the cabinet, and the potatoes in the cellar. You could leave a yellow balsam to blossom on the living room windowsill and look the cat in the eye. And towards evening, you could pull a chair to the window to watch how the mountains grow sombre and how the horizon starts to shine. The same radiance that burns within a fresh wound.

✺

Christmas is just a few days away, days that you love so much. The acer is calm and white. Alpine choughs land on its branches and the tree seems to come alive. The branches tremble and snow falls to the ground. In summer, the choughs are up by the cabin. Every day, they fly in and out of the valley, come to see if we have any morsels for them, and while we watch the chamois through our binoculars, their sharp cries cross the valley. But when winter arrives, they return to the village. It is good to know that there are even colder places out there when it is freezing. They have just flown over the rooftops; small black flickers. I am sure that one of them is now keeping watch somewhere. When I put out food, they appear a short while later, arriving from God knows where, flapping around and chirping and pecking, then they disappear. Sometimes, a solitary chough lingers on one of the acer's branches and looks towards the kitchen window. And the acer seems foreign to me.

THE KING

The King of the Orient has wrapped himself in purple fabric and is wearing a golden crown. With a devout countenance, he leaves the house and walks down the alley through the fresh snow. He reaches up and opens the doors. Hello, he cries into the buildings' hallways, and declares that a child was born in Bethlehem, a child who cannot be betrayed to Herod. The King of the Orient's language is foreign, the people do not understand it. Yet since he is a king, they all nod and invite him into the warmth to sit for a moment.

Later, the King returns up the alley. He walks down the corridor, opens the door to the living room and sits at the table without uttering a word. His crown shines under the lamplight.

※

Strange, how snoring becomes louder once you notice it. It gets louder and louder, saws thoughts and images in two. The clocktower surges above the rooftops outside in the night. The snow in the garden is heavy. There is snow on the roofs too. On the benches. On the stacked firewood. The windows of the house opposite are black squares. And then the acer is here, always here, appearing before the windows, stretching out into the air, bearing snow, foliating, forming seeds and dropping them.

At the corner of the house, the alley is bathed in a dim light. I watch how you walk up the steep lane into the sun, at first fast and then slow, taking breaks and then continuing onwards, murmuring to yourself, and when you disappear behind the corner, I am a little out of breath.

Down in the stable, a bull clatters and crashes about.

※

I walk up the path. Someone has trodden steps into the snow on the slope. They are a little crooked and I find it difficult to keep my balance. At the top of the hill, there are fresh tracks in the snow.

Now it is snowing again. The snowflakes are growing. Snow is falling on top of snow. How can you even believe in the sun among all this silent white? Your name on the wooden plaque has faded. The bunch of rowan berries held on for a long time. I like the colour of the rowan berries against the blue in autumn. You can still see the upright headstones clearly. Those that tilt backwards slightly have a confidence about them in summer, their gaze to the sky. If you light a candle, the light of the flame begins to dance on the church wall the moment it starts to get dark. Once, your candle burnt until early the next day, until the swallows began to fly.

    The cat that had taken a nap on the wall stretched out, cleaned herself and strolled away across the graves to the church.

    When I looked around, she was gone.

Someone said they saw you on the day of your funeral, sitting cross-legged on the ridge of our roof. You were watching the crowd and laughing. You waved to every single person and greeted them by name.

※

The ibex is up there, looking around. With his forelegs, he is standing on one mountain and with his hindlegs, he is standing on another. His horns are dark arches in the sky. On sunny days, he can see the sea glistening. Sometimes he will turn his head down towards the valley. He will just stand there, look around and chew grass.

TRANSLATOR'S NOTE

In *As if Nothing Were*, Rut Plouda explores the life of her son, Joannes, who had Down's Syndrome and passed away at the age of nineteen. He dreamed of being a shepherd, a sailor, a hunter, or a musician.

+SVIZRA is a series of eight chapbooks showcasing contemporary writing translated from the four official languages of Switzerland: German, French, Italian and Romansh. In giving equal visibility to each of the four languages, **+SVIZRA** offers a range of Swiss writing never before seen in English from a diverse group of some of the best authors living and working in Switzerland today, including National Literature Prize winning Anna Ruchat, Iraqi exile Usama Al-Shahmani and treasured Romansh author, Rut Plouda.

+SVIZRA is the result of Strangers Press' latest exciting collaboration with an international group of authors, translators, publishers, designers and editors, all made possible by generous funding from Pro Helvetia.

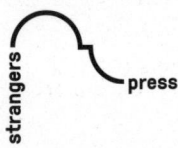

Supported By

University of East Anglia

NORWICH
UNIVERSITY
OF THE ARTS